Cash crazy!

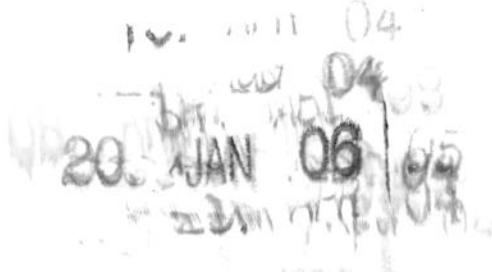

Millie and Bombassa

Make friends with the funniest duo in town!

 Be sure to read: 

Dizzy D.I.Y.!

... and lots, lots more!

Cash Crazy!

written and illustrated by

Shoo Rayner

SCHOLASTIC

Scholastic Children's Books,
Commonwealth House, 1-19 New Oxford Street,
London, WC1A 1NU, UK
a division of Scholastic Ltd
London ~ New York ~ Toronto ~ Sydney ~ Auckland
Mexico City ~ New Delhi ~ Hong Kong

First published by Scholastic Ltd, 2002

ISBN 0 439 99465 9

Printed and bound by Oriental Press, Dubai, UAE

10 9 8 7 6 5 4 3 2 1

Chapter One

Bombassa opened his eyes and pulled back the curtain. It was dull and grey outside.

"What a horrible, boring day," he thought. "I'd better stay in bed. I'll just have a bit of breakfast first."

Bombassa got up, made a huge cup of tea and headed straight back to bed.

He reached beside the bed and took two huge biscuits from a tin. Then he dunked them in his tea, spilling crumbs and drips all over the duvet.

As soon as Bombassa had finished his breakfast, he snuggled back down.

He was just beginning to feel sleepy again, when he heard the front gate click. It was the postman.

Bombassa listened to him walk up the path, and push some things through the letterbox.

"Ha!" said Bombassa. "I bet they're bills. That's all I ever get. Bills, bills, bills!"

He was just drifting into a lovely dream, when a little voice twittered in his ear.

"Wakey, wakey! Rise and shine! Look what came in the post."

It was Millie, Bombassa's best friend. She was clutching the post in her beak.

"Three bills!" moaned Bombassa, as he tossed them on the floor.

"A gift catalogue that I can't afford to look at. And what's this?"

He held up a bright red envelope and examined the bold, swirly writing on the front.

Bombassa moaned, "Oh no! It's from Auntie Daz. She thinks I'm a lazy good for nothing who never gets out of bed. She only ever writes when she's cross with me. I'll open it later."

But Millie couldn't bear to see a letter unopened. She wanted to know what was inside.

"It might be important," said Millie. "Maybe she's getting married?"

Bombassa rolled his eyes. "Ha! Who'd marry her? She's far too bossy."

"Maybe she's been ill?"

Bombassa pulled the pillow over his head. "She's as fit as a fiddle. As strong as an ox!"

"Maybe she's sent you some holiday photos?"

Bombassa hid under the duvet. "I've already got a photo of her. I don't need any more!"

Millie tried again. "Well, maybe…"

Bombassa sighed. "All right, all right! I give in!" He picked up the envelope and ripped it open.

Chapter Two

Bombassa looked more closely at the envelope. Folded inside was a crisp, new ten pound note!

Bombassa leaped into the air, twirled three times and danced across the bedroom.

He picked up Auntie Daz's photo and gave it a great big kiss.

"Ten pounds! My favourite auntie! What a dear … what shall I spend it on?"

"You don't have to spend it straight away," said Millie, looking at the brown envelopes on the floor. "You could pay one of those bills."

"Nonsense!" roared Bombassa. "Auntie Daz wants me to buy something wonderful!"

In no time at all, he was dressed and ready to go shopping. He stuffed the ten pound note in his pocket.

Bombassa turned to Millie, "I'm off to the shops!" he said. "Are you coming with me?"

"I suppose so," sighed Millie. "Someone's got to keep an eye on you!"

Bombassa slammed the door and swaggered off down the road with Millie sitting on his shoulder.

Chapter Three

"What shall I buy?" sang Bombassa, excitedly. "What shall I buy?"

Millie thought he needed some good advice.

"You don't have to spend it," she said again. "You could put it in the bank and save up for something big."

"Fiddlesticks!" roared Bombassa. "Auntie Daz wants me to buy something wonderful, so I shall!"

Millie rolled her eyes. Nothing could stop Bombassa when he set his mind to something.

Soon, the two friends were outside Henry's Toy Store.

Bombassa barged through the doors. "This is the place for me!" he said.

It was like heaven inside! There were toys everywhere. Lights flashed, robots whirred, trains chuff-chuffed.

Bombassa looked around excitedly. "I think we should start in the basement and work our way up. Come on!"

He rushed downstairs to the music and electronic departments.

"Look at all these cool games," Bombassa said to Millie. "I'd really like one of those racing car games. I'd be really happy if I had one of those."

"But you won't get one for ten pounds, will you?" said Millie. "If you put your money in the bank, you could save up for one."

Bombassa didn't answer. He raced over to the music department and…

"Maybe I could afford a keyboard," he said. "Look, here's the very thing!"

He picked up a tiny keyboard and turned it on. A horrid, screechy, crackling beat came out of it.

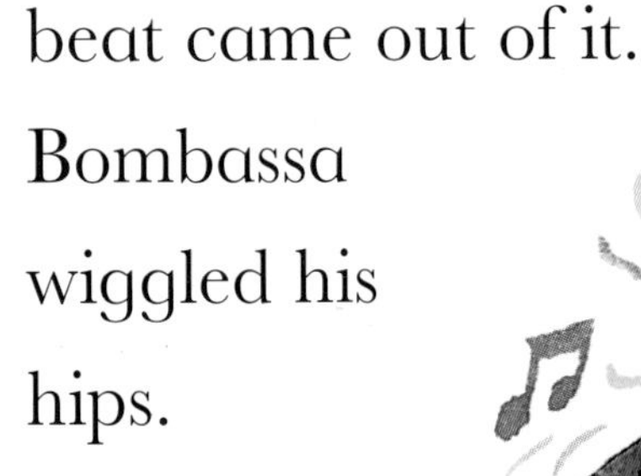

Bombassa wiggled his hips.

"It doesn't sound very good," said Millie.

Bombassa smiled. "But it's got loads of buttons and it's only ten pounds, so I can afford it."

Millie pointed to the price ticket. In tiny writing it read: batteries not included.

"You can't afford the batteries as well," she said.

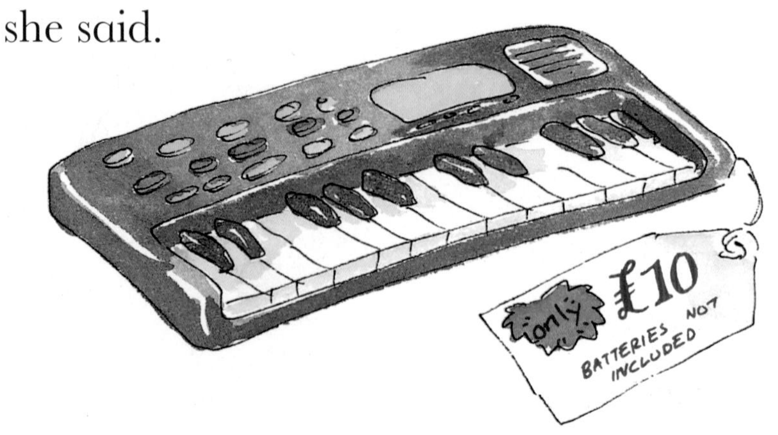

Bombassa sighed and looked all around. All he could afford was a drumstick...

...or a cybertorch with red and green flashing safety lights...

...or a mug that played tunes when you picked it up.

"Come on," said Millie. "You can't play the drums. You've got six torches at home and that mug is much too small for you! Let's look somewhere else."

Chapter Four

They got into the lift and went up to the gift and gadget department. As the lift doors opened, Bombassa's face lit up.

"This is the place for me," he boomed.

Everywhere you looked, the shelves were full of completely useless things. Bombassa thought it was all wonderful!

"Look at this!" he exclaimed as he tossed a coin in the air. He caught it and smacked it on the back of his wrist.

The coin said "YES"!

"It's a mind maker-upper!" he said. "It says "NO" on the other side. I really want to buy it … I can afford it."

Millie rolled her eyes. "You silly twit! You can use any old coin for that."

But Bombassa wasn't listening. He had found something else already. "Look at this … it's a calculator made to look like a cow! It's called a Cowculator, get it? I must have it."

Millie sighed. "You've already got a calculator at home. Why don't you stick a pair of horns on that instead?"

But Bombassa didn't answer. He'd already found something else. It was a blow-up chair that looked like a desert island with its own palm tree. "What a great chair!" Bombassa whooped, as he sat down.

There was a loud pop and a hissing sound.

The desert island began to lose its puff...

...and the palm tree flopped to the floor.

"Quick!" said Millie. "Let's get out of here."

They leaped into the lift and pressed the button for the dressing-up department on the next floor.

Bombassa tried on a spacesuit. "Hey, do I look cool in this, or what?"

He walked up and down in front of the mirror.

Then he looked at the price.

"If you put your money in the bank—"
Millie began to say.

"Yeah, yeah!" Bombassa grumbled. "I could save up until I could afford it. But Auntie Daz wants me to buy something wonderful!"

Millie waited while Bombassa tried on all sorts of costumes and disguises.

Cowboy hats.

False beards.

A doctor's outfit.

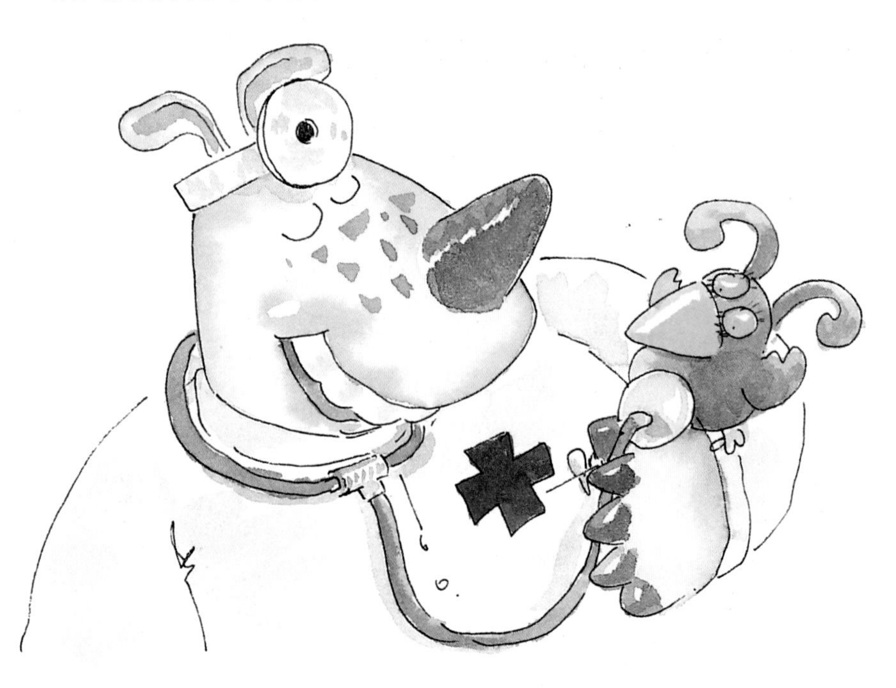

A twirling bow tie.

All he could afford was a pair of curly-wurly, joke shoelaces.

Bombassa gave Millie a hopeful look. "I could buy these," he said.

"But you don't even wear shoes!" said Millie.

Chapter Five

They trailed over to look at the store guide by the lift. Bombassa saw that there was a restaurant on the top floor.

"Phew!" said Bombassa. "All this shopping is making me hungry! Do you think Auntie Daz would mind if I spent my money on a really good meal?"

"If you think that would be something wonderful," said Millie, "I suppose it would be all right. Still, I really think you should save it for..."

But Bombassa was already in the lift.

In the restaurant, he ordered a double Jungle Deluxe with double cheese, double fries and a double thick milkshake for himself, and a seedburger for Millie.

"That will be five pounds and twenty-three pence, please," said the nice antelope behind the counter.

Bombassa reached into his pocket. But the ten pound note wasn't there!

"Where can it be?" said Bombassa, beginning to panic. He looked in every pocket, but it wasn't in any of them.

The nice antelope gave them a long, hard stare. He tore up their order and said, "Who's next!"

Millie was very cross. "How many times have I told you to put your money in a wallet? Or even better, put it in the bank."

Tired and hungry, they searched in all the places they had been. But nobody had found Bombassa's ten pound note.

"My ten pounds must have fallen out of my pocket," cried Bombassa. "I bet someone found it and kept it... Someone's had a lucky day."

Slowly, they trailed home.

Chapter Six

Bombassa opened the front door and stepped inside. His foot trod on something crisp and crunchy.

"Look!" chirped Millie. "It's your ten pound note! It must have fallen out of your pocket. It's been lying on the mat all along!"

Bombassa hugged the ten pound note and laughed with relief. Then he went straight to the kitchen and made a big cup of tea.

"I suppose you'll want to go back to the shops and spend it now?" asked Millie.

"No," said Bombassa. "I'm going back to bed where I should have stayed this morning."

As he dunked biscuits in his tea, crumbs and drips fell all over the duvet.

Millie picked at the crumbs. "Well, are you going to put the money in the bank, then?" she asked.

Bombassa smiled at her and opened the glossy gift catalogue that had come in the post that morning.

Millie sighed. She knew that Bombassa would never save his money, so she sat on his shoulder and looked through the catalogue with him.

"Oh!" she said pointing to a pen that could write upside down. "That's nice … and you can afford it!"